Brady Brady
Teammate Turnaround

Written by Mary Shaw
Illustrated by Chuck Temple

Scholastic Canada Ltd.
Toronto   New York   London   Auckland   Sydney
Mexico City   New Delhi   Hong Kong   Buenos Aires

Scholastic Canada Ltd.
604 King Street West, Toronto, Ontario M5V 1E1, Canada

Scholastic Inc.
557 Broadway, New York, NY 10012, USA

Scholastic Australia Pty Limited
PO Box 579, Gosford, NSW 2250, Australia

Scholastic New Zealand Limited
Private Bag 94407, Botany, Manukau 2163, New Zealand

Scholastic Children's Books
Euston House, 24 Eversholt Street, London NW1 1DB, UK

www.scholastic.ca

Library and Archives Canada Cataloguing in Publication

Title: Teammate turnaround / written by Mary Shaw ; illustrated by Chuck Temple.

Names: Shaw, Mary, 1965- author. | Temple, Chuck, 1962- illustrator.

Description: Series statement: Brady Brady

Identifiers: Canadiana 2018906658X | ISBN 9781443163736 (hardcover) | ISBN 9781443163750 (softcover)

Classification: LCC PS8587.H3473 T44 2019 | DDC jC813/.6—dc23

6 5 4 3 2 1   Printed in Malaysia   108   19 20 21 22 23

To my fave nieces, Owyn and Ellie. My Yukon beauties.
— Mary Shaw

To the best teammate ever . . . my wife, Laura.
— Chuck Temple

Brady loved hockey. Hockey was all Brady thought about. He thought about it so much that everyone had to call him twice to get his attention.

It drove his family **_crrrazy_**!

"Brady, Brady! Take Hatrick for a walk."
"Brady, Brady! Air out your hockey bag."
"Brady, Brady! Time for bed."

Pretty soon they just called him Brady Brady.
It was easier that way.

Brady and his buddy Chester met at Brady's house.
They had been practicing for weeks to get ready for
hockey sort outs.

"I can't wait to have the team all together again,"
Brady shouted as he took a shot. "The Icehogs are
going to have the best year ever!"

"I hope so," said Chester. "I always get butterflies before sort outs. And games. And sometimes even practices."

The boys played until dinnertime. "I'll see you at the rink first thing tomorrow," Brady said, high-fiving Chester.

That night, Brady was so excited he slept in his equipment.

He was the first one at the rink in the morning and high-fived his friends as they arrived.

"The Icehogs are together again!" said Brady excitedly.

"Can we have a team cheer for good luck?" Chester asked, wringing his hands.

"We've got the power,
We've got the might,
We've got the spirit . . .

*. . . **Sort outs will be outta sight!**"*

When they got on the ice, everyone skated as fast as they could. Brady got to take a few shots on Chester, and he tapped Chester's goalie pads for good luck each time he skated past him.

Chester made some wicked saves.

After the skate, the kids waited nervously
for their turn to meet with the coaches
and find out which team they were on.

Brady got good news — he was an Icehog again!
Brady waited outside for Chester. He was so excited
about playing with his friend.

When Chester finally came out, he had pulled his hat down over his face. He walked right past Brady without saying a word.

Brady watched as Chester dumped his goalie equipment at the front of the arena, along with a piece of paper that read:

Free equipment. No longer needed.

Chester got in his dad's car. Brady had never seen him so sad.

"What's going on? Why are you giving away your stuff?" Brady asked.

"I'm quitting hockey!" Chester steamed. "I didn't get put on the Icehogs. If I can't play with my friends, I don't want to play at all."

Brady's heart sank. He was really sad that he and Chester weren't on the same team, but he knew he had to cheer up his friend.

Brady climbed in beside Chester. "You'll still be my best buddy forever. We're gonna win the Stanley Cup together one day, remember?"

At the mention of the Stanley Cup, Chester looked thoughtful.

Brady kept going. "It doesn't matter that we aren't on the same team. We can still play hockey together. On my backyard rink, in my basement, on my driveway. And besides, you can't quit. You *love* playing hockey!"

"**Well** . . . I do like to make a save," admitted Chester. He hustled out of his car and raced to the front of the arena.

Chester stopped at the bottom step.

He felt sick to his stomach. His equipment was *gone!*

Chester was crushed. "I guess I really won't be playing hockey after all."

Then Brady noticed a group of kids in the lobby. "Maybe they've seen something," he said. "Let's go ask."

"Hi, guys. I'm Brady, and this is my friend Chester. He's a goalie. We're looking for his equipment."

"I . . . uh . . . left it by the doors and it's gone! I really need it back!" explained Chester.

"Sorry. I haven't seen anything," said the tallest kid.

"But we can help you look," said the smallest kid.

They looked in every
dressing room.

Nothing.

They looked in
the washroom.

Nothing.

They looked in the
concession stand.

Nothing.

"We've looked **everywhere**," moaned Chester. "I'll never get my stuff back."

"We can't give up," said Brady. "You need to play hockey."

"How about we check the lost and found?" suggested the tallest kid.

"My mom says it's the last place anyone looks," added the smallest kid.

The lost and found was located in a dark storage room. Brady had never seen so much stuff crammed into one place.

They peered into the darkness of the lost and found. There, high up on a shelf, was Chester's goalie gear. **Really** high up.

Chester climbed the shelf and fell backwards into a pile of clothes.

Brady stood on a hockey bag, but he wasn't tall enough.

Chester jumped onto Brady's shoulders. But they still couldn't reach Chester's stuff.

"We're not giving up yet," cried Brady. "I have an idea!"

Everyone huddled together to listen to Brady's plan.

The kids formed a human pyramid.
Chester climbed on top.

Chester reached and reached
some more. His fingers **barely**
touched the straps of his
goalie pads.

He yanked, and the pads dropped to the ground with a big thud.

Everyone cheered. Chester hugged his goalie pads and beamed. That was when he noticed the kids' jerseys.

"Hey!" Chester cried excitedly. "That's the team I got placed on."

"Awesome!" said the smallest kid.

"Welcome to the Rattlers," said the tallest kid. "We need a great goalie!"

Chester's new team chanted:

*"Rink Rattlers, bite the ice,
Teamwork makes us twice as nice!"*

Chester high-fived his new friends.

The first game of the season was the Icehogs against the Rink Rattlers.

As he skated to the net, Chester waved at his old friends on the Icehogs' bench, and his new ones on the Rink Rattlers' bench. It felt good to be on the ice. Chester knew it didn't matter what uniform he was wearing as long as he was playing the sport he loved.